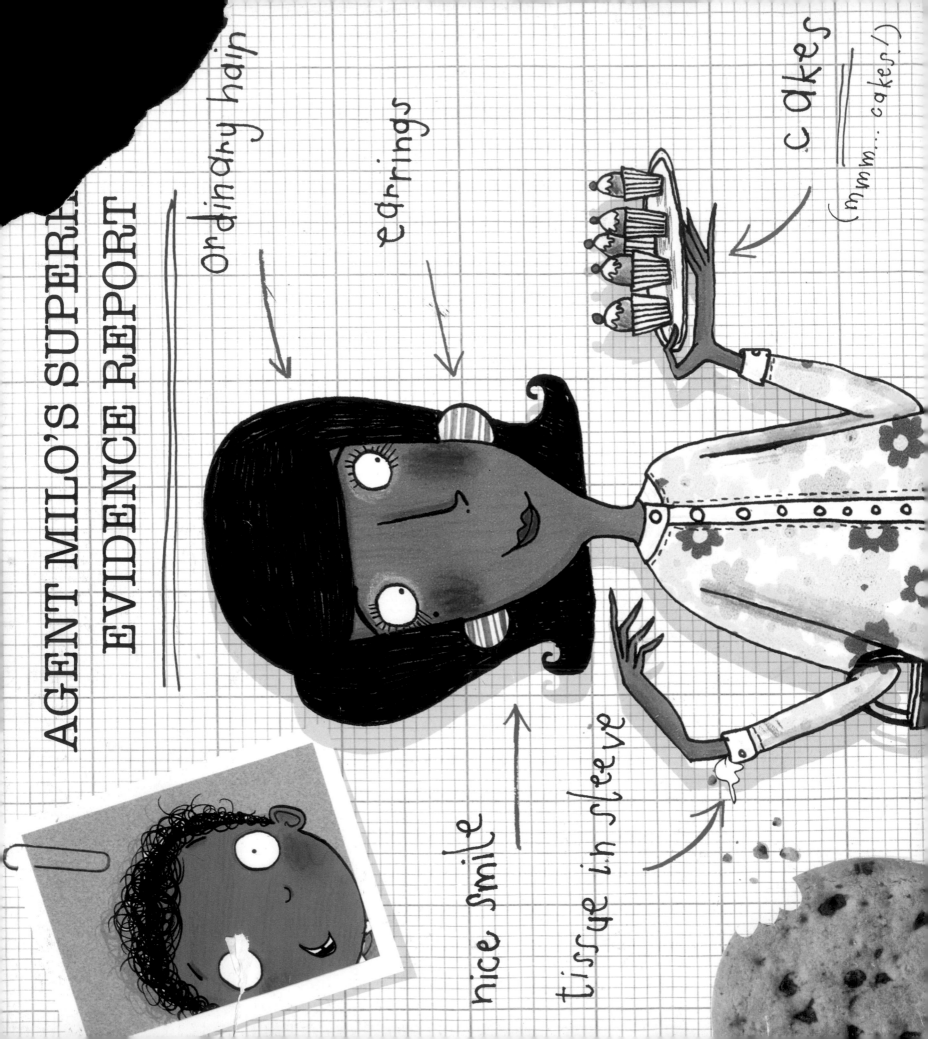

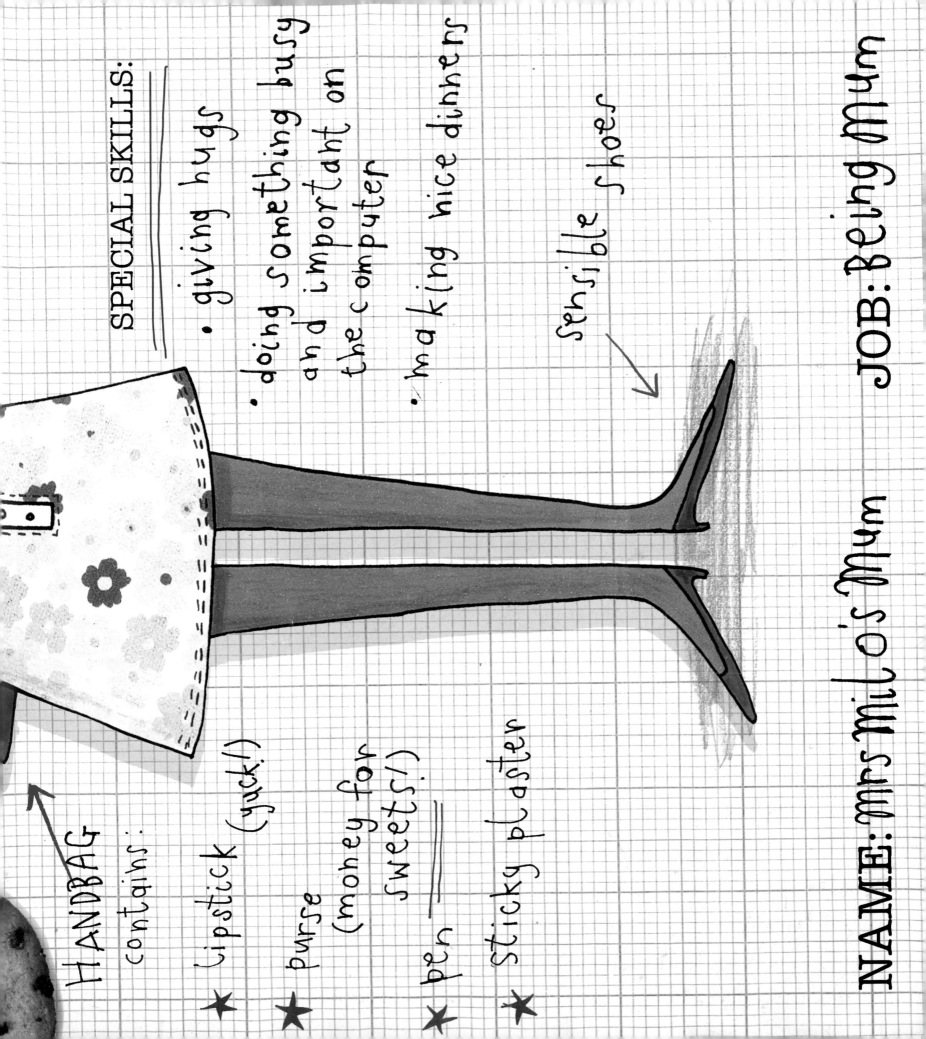

SPECIAL SKILLS:

- giving hugs
- doing something busy and important on the computer
- making nice dinners

sensible shoes

HANDBAG contains:

★ lipstick (yuck!)

★ purse (money for sweets!)

★ pen

★ sticky plaster

NAME: Mrs Milo's Mum

JOB: Being Mum

For the House of Handley:
Jill, Brian and Jennifer
(and of course Ben and Bert the cats!)
A.T.S.

For my Supermum!
A.M.

THE GOSSIP

This edition published in 2016
First published in 2010 as *My Mum Has X-Ray Vision*
by Scholastic Children's Books, Euston House, 24 Eversholt Street, London NW1 1DB
a division of Scholastic Ltd
www.scholastic.co.uk

London ~ New York ~ Toronto ~ Sydney ~ Auckland ~ Mexico City ~ New Delhi ~ Hong Kong

Text copyright © 2010 Angela McAllister · Illustrations copyright © 2010 Alex T. Smith

My Mum Is a Supermum

Angela McAllister

Alex T. Smith

SCHOLASTIC

MILO'S MUM was like all the other mums. She had ordinary hair, ordinary clothes and a nice smile.

MILO'S MUM was just like all the other mums…

EXCEPT she could see through things. Milo was pretty sure she had

X-RAY VISION.

On Monday, he was wrestling with a **GIANT SEA MONSTER** when **MUM** shouted from downstairs.

"MILO! SIT DOWN IN THE BATH!"

How did she know what he was doing?

On Wednesday, he was brewing up spells in a mountain cave to defeat a **POWERFUL WIZARD** when **MUM** yelled from the kitchen.

"**MILO!** DON'T USE MY **SAUCEPANS** IN THE **GARDEN!**"

How did she know
that he had them?

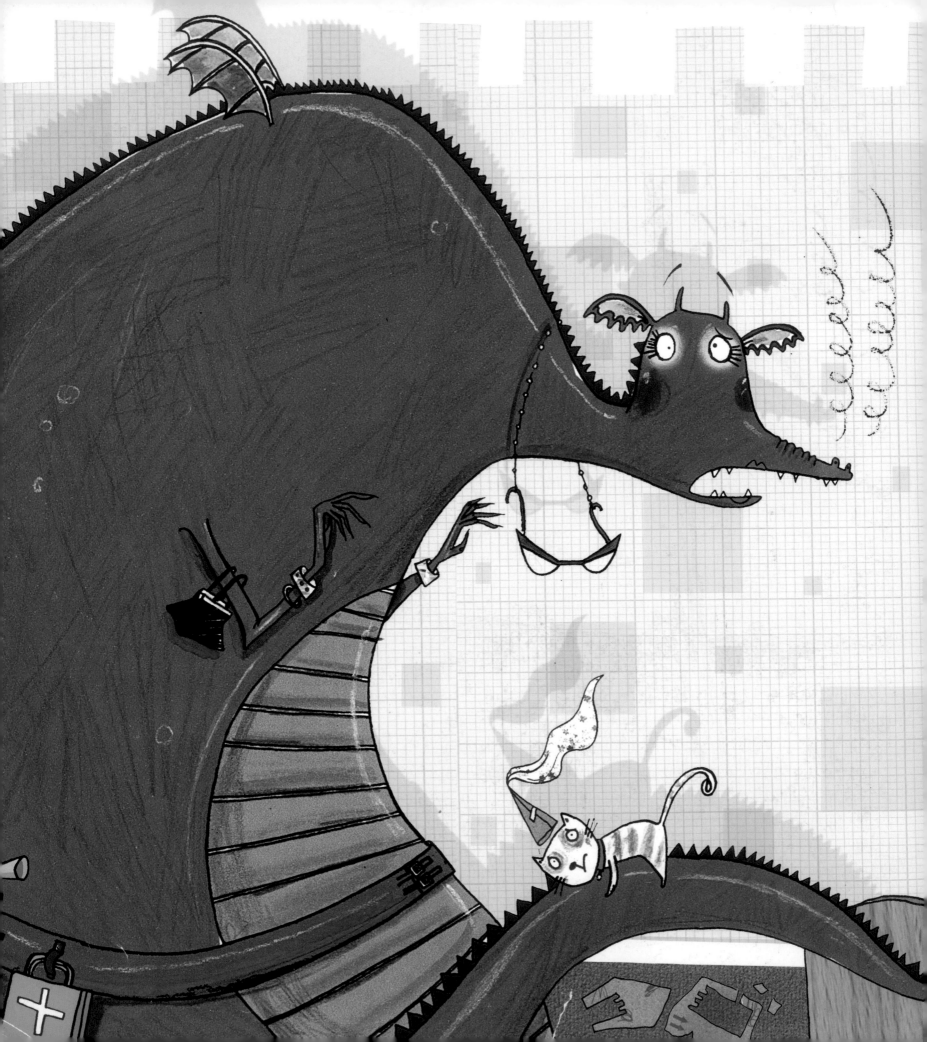

On Friday, he was defending his castle from an **ENORMOUS FIRE-BREATHING DRAGON**, when **MUM** called up from the sitting room.

"MILO! DON'T BOUNCE ON THE BED!"

How did she know where he was?

Thump!

"It's really weird," Milo said to his friend Lola. "My **MUM** can see what I'm doing when she isn't there. She must have **X-RAY VISION**."

...like a superhero!

Wow!

"I'll ask my brother," said Lola. "He's always reading **SUPERHERO** comics. He'll know about **X-RAY VISION**."

But Milo had to find out for himself. "I'll give **MUM** a test," he thought.

On Saturday, when **MUM** asked him to help bring in the shopping, Milo crept upstairs and hid in the wardrobe.

"**MILO!**" called **MUM**. "**WHERE ARE YOU GOING?**"

Milo smiled to himself.
  "If **MUM** comes right inside, right up the stairs, right into the bedroom, and opens the wardrobe door, then I'll know for sure that she has **X-RAY VISION**."

Milo waited.
But **MUM** didn't come.

Aargh!

Milo waited.
Still **MUM** didn't come.
Maybe she couldn't see
through wardrobes...

Still Milo waited.
Maybe **MUM** couldn't
see through doors…

"Maybe **MUM** has forgotten me," thought Milo.

Then suddenly he heard footsteps. Someone came up the stairs. Someone opened the door. **"MUM!"** called Milo and out he jumped.

But it wasn't **MUM**.

Lola offered Milo a gumdrop. "My brother says
that mums never have **X-RAY VISION**," she said.
"And he knows."

"He's right," sighed Milo. "I was wrong.
I hid but she couldn't find me.
She's **NOT** a **SUPERHERO**.
She's just an ordinary **MUM**, like all the rest."

Then they heard a
rustle in the hall.

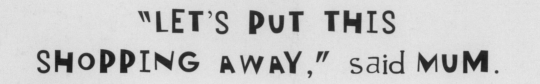

"LET'S PUT THIS SHOPPING AWAY," said MUM.

So Milo and Lola helped **MUM**, and she thanked them with her nice, ordinary smile.

"Come on, Lola," said Milo,
"let's make a den now."
But just as they made a dash
for the door…
"MILO!" shouted **MUM.**
**"DON'T HIDE THAT PACKET
OF CRISPS UP YOUR JUMPER!"**

Milo looked at **MUM** suspiciously. Then
a big grin crept onto his face.
"Guess what?" he whispered to Lola.

NAME: SUPERMUM JOB: Saving the World!

Rocket boots

DRAMATIC RESCUE: Supermum rescues her neighbour Mrs Ethel Hogsbottom who fell from her bedroom

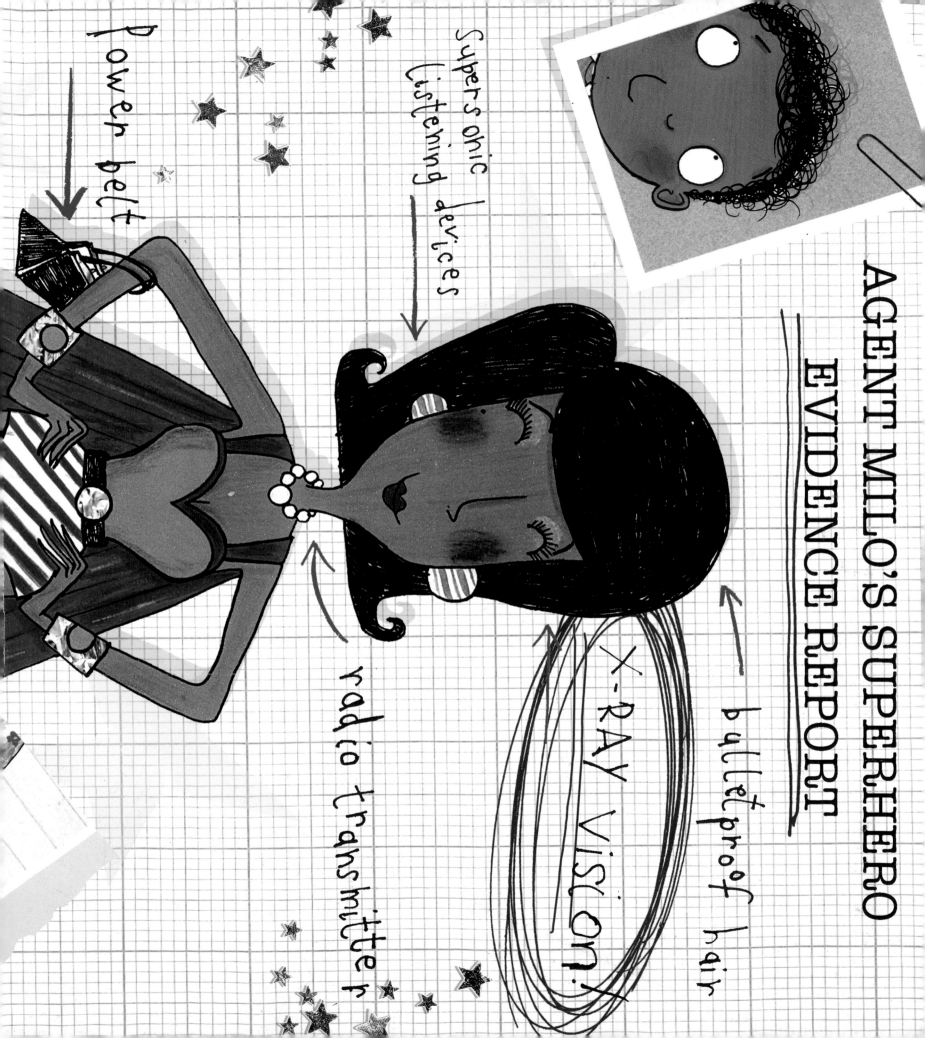

THE END